The Goblin Baby

Lauren Mills

Dial Books for Young Readers New York

Gerta

The Gnomes

Ralph

Fritz

Edna

Amanda with Miss Lucy Larkin and Turnip

I work in the garden with Miss Lucy Larkin. I pull up the weeds and she eats the dandelion greens. We like to play hide-and-seek, and sometimes old Turnip, my neighbor's dog, joins us. Turnip always finds Miss Lucy in the cabbage patch, where she is NOT supposed to go. Miss Lucy Larkin does not much care for Turnip, so he is politely asked to leave. Then we call on our garden friends, the gnomes.

The gnomes like to ride on Miss Lucy's back, but she doesn't mind. They are very helpful to us in many ways. If Miss Lucy has a queasy stomach from eating too much, they feed her chamomile petals.

The gnomes are not always kind, though. When they find a toad they will poke it with a twig just to make it hop, and then they laugh at it. They call the toads names like "warty-head" and "jelly belly." But I scold them and say, "It's not nice to tease. You must *always* be kind to someone smaller than yourself."

Then the gnomes hang their heads low in shame, and usually Fritz or maybe Gerta will pick a flower and give it to me. "We're sorry, Amanda," they say.

I tell them, "You should be apologizing to the poor little toads, not to *me*." But speaking nicely to toads is something they will never, ever do.

Lately I have been in the garden a lot with Miss Lucy Larkin. Mama has a new baby, my brother. He can't do a thing for himself and takes up all of Mama's time. My garden friends want to see him, but I'm afraid they will think he's as ugly as a toad. He certainly does not look a thing like ME. He is pink and wrinkly with little bumps, and when he cries he looks just like a toad squirming on its back.

Sometimes I wonder if he is my brother at all. Maybe he is not. Maybe some goblin has stolen away my *real* brother and put a changeling that looks just like him in my brother's place. I am frightened thinking about this, and the gnomes are worried too. We decide not to tell Miss Lucy Larkin, not yet.

I watch the next time Mama brings the baby into the garden. When the sun hits his eyes he squirms and cries. My friends look him over and nod sadly.

"Is it true?" I ask.

"Yes," they say. "This baby cannot be your real brother. He must be a changeling, most probably a goblin baby. You see?" They point. "He even cries in the sunshine, and have you *ever* seen him smile?"

I shake my head no and decide I will no longer touch this goblin baby.

Miss Lucy has heard the gnomes talking, and now she is very worried. A goblin baby will certainly pull her ears or squeeze her neck. After she sniffs the baby, she shakes herself from head to tail and hops away. I wish *I* could hop away.

Mama wants to know why I turn my back on the baby, but I can't bring myself to tell her the sad news. The gnomes want me to be happy again. Fritz says we should think of a way to find my real brother and bring him back. He is right.

I decide to hold a meeting with the gnomes and Miss Lucy Larkin. Fritz, Gerta, Ralph, and Edna agree to help me. Our plan is this: Tonight when the moon is high the gnomes will unlock Miss Lucy's cage, then ride like the dickens across the meadow, over the wooden bridge, through the woods, and up Turkey Hill, where there is a passageway to the Queen of the Earth's castle. They will offer gifts to the queen, then ask her to exchange the babies.

I gather gifts for the Queen of the Earth: a lace doily Grandma made, a birthday candle from my sixth birthday, a thimble, my first loose tooth that I refused to give to the tooth fairy, dried roses and lavender from the garden. I also make a drawing of myself and the baby, so that the queen will know who the gnomes are talking about.

After dinner I look out the window and notice that something is wrong. The gnomes won't be able to open Miss Lucy's cage, because I've forgotten to put the ramp up to her door! It's getting dark, but I sneak outside and quickly fix the ramp.

Oh, oh . . . oh, no. What is THAT coming toward me? It's much too big and hairy to be a gnome, and its eyes are glowing green just like a goblin's—a goblin that might steal a medium-sized girl!

I run to the house, yelling, "Goblin, go away! You took my brother, but you can't have ME!" Then I trip, and its slimy wet tongue touches my face. Its tail wags. It's Turnip!

"Go home!" I scold him. Turnip is sad, so I pat his head before I run back inside. The goblin baby is squealing, so Mama hasn't even noticed I was almost stolen away. I look out the window and whisper, "Run like the dickens, Miss Lucy Larkin!"

In the morning I rush out to see Miss Lucy. She is looking awfully peaked, so I let her rest. I go to the garden and call the gnomes. They come out sleepily. Fritz wants to talk first.

"Imagine it," he says. "The Queen of the Earth and all her royal fairies were there waiting just for *us*."

"Did the Queen of the Earth like my gifts?" I ask.

"Oh, yes," he tells me.

"And will she exchange the babies?" I want to know, but the gnomes look away and scratch their heads.

Edna says, "It is a very delicate matter, you see, because the queen herself does not have the real baby. The goblins have your brother, and they are just too tricky to mess with. Now it's time for us to go back to bed."

I put my head in my hands and am about to cry, but the little gnomes tug at my hair and try to pull my fingers away from my eyes. They do all their silly tricks to try to get me to smile, but I will not.

Then Gerta says, "There, there, don't worry, Amanda. The Queen of the Earth is very powerful, and she will do all she can to make the goblins obey."

"Yes," says Ralph, "and she told us that you will know that they have returned your baby brother when you see him smile. Goblin babies *never* smile."

The four gnomes yawn and say they must go to bed at once. I thank them for all the hard work they have done for me and give them each a button, their most favorite thing.

For many, many days I try to make the baby smile. I make my funniest faces and silliest voices, but he is still a goblin baby. I wish those goblins would take him back.

"Something must be wrong," I finally tell the gnomes. "The baby still won't smile. There must be more we can do."

"Nothing I can think of," says Ralph, and the others say, "Nope, nope, nothing at all." But Miss Lucy Larkin thumps angrily on the ground and scowls at them. The gnomes hang their heads, and I know there's something they are keeping from me.

I say, "I cannot be your friend if you're not truthful. What is it you aren't telling me?"

By and by they tell me what else the Queen of the Earth had said, but it is very, very hard for them.

They tell me that the toads they tease are really baby gnomes who are learning about the garden and the earth by being toads first, and that THEY all had been toads once as well, but none of them could remember such a stinky thing.

They are quiet, then Gerta says, "The Queen of the Earth wants us to be kind and patient with the toads so that they will grow into *good* gnomes someday. When we learn to treat the toads nicely, the real baby will be returned."

"Then we must start right away," I tell them. And now they are giving the toads drinks of water in acorn shells. They are even speaking nicely to the toads without making faces. I am very proud of those gnomes!

I am trying to be kind and patient with the goblin baby too, just in case he is my real brother.

One afternoon Mama brings the baby to the garden and puts him on my lap. Miss Lucy and the gnomes watch from under the leaves to see what will happen.

At first the baby begins to fuss. I speak softly to him and he settles down. Miss Lucy Larkin hops over to us and sniffs him. He tries to grab her ears, but I hold his little hand out and let him gently touch her fur.

And all at once—HE SMILES! Mama and I both laugh, the gnomes cheer, and Miss Lucy leaps into the air with a twist!

At last he *is* my baby brother. And I bet those goblins are glad to have their own baby back. If there's one thing goblins can't stand, it's a smiling baby!

For "The Little Man"

With appreciation for the inspirational lives of Sulamith Wulfing and Opal Whitely

Published by Dial Books for Young Readers
A division of Penguin Putnam Inc.
345 Hudson Street / New York, New York 10014

Printed in Hong Kong on acid-free paper
First Edition
1 3 5 7 9 10 8 6 4 2

Library of Congress Cataloging in Publication Data
Mills, Lauren A.
The goblin baby / by Lauren Mills.—1st ed.   p.   cm.
Summary: Because she is reluctant to accept her new baby brother, Amanda convinces her garden
friends that a goblin has stolen her real sibling and replaced him with a changeling.
ISBN 0-8037-2172-2
[1. Brothers and sisters—Fiction. 2. Babies—Fiction. 3. Jealousy—Fiction. 4. Imagination—Fiction.] I. Title.
PZ7.M63979Go   1999
[E]—dc21   98-10971   CIP   AC

The artwork was rendered in watercolors.